The Final Problem

By Arthur Conan Doyle
Adapted by David Eastman
Illustrated by Allan Eitzen

TROLL ASSOCIATES

Library of Congress Cataloging in Publication Data

Eastman, David.
    Sherlock Holmes—The final problem.

    Summary: Sherlock Holmes strives to destroy
Professor Moriarty who is at the bottom of half
the evil in London while the criminal genius vows
the same for the detective.
    [1. Mystery and detective stories]   I. Eitzen,
Allan, ill.   II. Doyle, Arthur Conan, Sir, 1859-
1930. Final problem.   III. Title.   IV. Title:
Final problem.
PZ7.E1269Fi   [Fic]   81-11609
ISBN-0-89375-612-1   AACR2
ISBN-0-89375-613-X (pbk.)

Printed in the United States of America
10 9 8 7 6 5 4 3 2 1

My heart is heavy as I think about the final problem faced by my friend, Mr. Sherlock Holmes. It began when he walked into my office on the evening of April twenty-fourth. He looked even thinner and paler than usual.

"Good evening, Dr. Watson," he said. "May I close your shutters?"

"You are afraid of something?" I asked.

"I simply recognize danger when it is near," he replied. "You have probably never heard of Professor Moriarty. He is at the bottom of half the evil in London. He is a criminal genius, who plans crimes that others carry out for him.

"For months, I tried to get enough evidence to convict him," explained my friend. "At last he made a slip, and I moved in. I have woven my net tighter and tighter, until it is now ready to be pulled closed. In three days—on Monday—the professor and his gang will be in the hands of the police.

"The only hope for the professor is to try to silence me before the trial. This morning, Moriarty appeared at my door. He is a tall man, with deeply sunken eyes. His face moves from side to side like a reptile's. He said that I was getting too close and would have to back off. I politely refused.

"He said that I was standing in the way of a mighty organization, and if I did not step aside, I would be stepped upon. I replied that I was determined to destroy him. He told me that he would not rest until he had done the same to me. Then he turned and strode out the door."

"Good heavens, Holmes!" I cried. "Has he tried to carry out his threat?"

"So far, his agents have tried three times," Holmes replied. "Around noon, a two-horse cart whizzed around a corner and was upon me in a flash. I leaped aside, and barely saved myself from being trampled to death. The horses raced off and were gone in an instant.

8

"Then, as I walked down the sidewalk, a brick came tumbling down from the roof of one of the houses. It shattered to fragments at my feet. The police searched the building and said that the wind must have toppled the brick. I knew better, but I could prove nothing. So I took a cab to my brother's rooms, where I spent the day.

"This evening, on my way here, I was attacked by a man with a club. I believe I am not safe in England until Professor Moriarty is behind bars. If you are free for a few days, Watson, I should very much like you to go with me to Paris."

"Certainly," I replied.

"Excellent," he said. "Send your luggage to Victoria Station tonight by messenger.

"Tomorrow," continued Holmes, "take a cab to the Arcade, but do not take the first cab you see. The minute your cab stops, dash through the Arcade, timing yourself to reach the other side at 9:15. A certain carriage will meet you and take you to Victoria Station. There we will meet inside the second first-class car on the train."

Holmes slipped out my back door and climbed over the garden wall. I heard him whistle for a cab, and then he was gone. In the morning, I followed his instructions. I had no trouble finding the exact train car, for it was marked "Occupied." But there was no sign of Holmes.

I helped an old man with his luggage and looked again for
Holmes. The old man climbed into our car and sat down. I told
him it was taken, but he did not understand much English.
Finally, I gave up and continued to look for my friend.
Something must have gone wrong. Already the doors had been
shut, and the train's whistle was blowing.

"My dear Watson," said the voice of Sherlock Holmes, "you have not even said good morning."

I spun around and stared in astonishment at the old man. I now realized that he was not an old man at all. He was Holmes, in one of his many disguises.

"Good heavens," I cried. "How you startled me!"

"Every precaution is still necessary," whispered Holmes. As the train began to move, he exclaimed, "Look! There is Moriarty!" A tall man was furiously pushing through the crowd and waving his hand, as if he wanted to stop the train. But it was too late. A moment later, we pulled away from the station.

Holmes removed his disguise and said, "Moriarty will take the next train and try to catch us at the end of the line. So we shall get off before then and make a cross-country trip to Newhaven. There, we can catch a boat to France. Professor Moriarty will then try to catch us in Paris, when we pick up our baggage. So instead of going to Paris, we will travel to Switzerland without our bags!"

We got off at the Canterbury station, and our train went on with our luggage. Holmes pointed back down the tracks toward a distant puff of smoke. It was the next train. "Moriarty will be on it," he said. We hid behind some boxes, and Moriarty's train roared by us.

At Newhaven, we caught a boat that took us across the channel to France. On Monday, Holmes telegraphed the London police. That evening, a reply was waiting at our hotel.

"They have arrested the entire gang," announced Holmes, "but Moriarty has escaped. He will not rest until he has tracked me down and had his revenge. I suggest you return to London, Watson, for I will be a dangerous companion now."

Of course, I refused to leave. We spent a week traveling through Switzerland. It was a lovely trip, through green valleys and over snow-capped mountains. But Holmes did not let down his guard for a moment. He knew that danger might lie at any turn.

Once, as we walked along the edge of a deep mountain lake, a large rock somehow broke free and fell from the ridge above us. It crashed down close behind us and roared into the lake. Falling rocks were common at that time of year, but Holmes knew at once that this one had been caused by Moriarty.

In an instant, he raced up the ridge. Standing on the highest point, he looked about in every direction, but saw no one.

"I tell you, Watson," he said, "if I could put an end to the career of Professor Moriarty, I would cheerfully bring my own career to a close."

It was early May when we reached a little village in central Switzerland. We stayed in the English House—a small hotel that was owned by a man who had once been a waiter in London. He suggested that we stop at the nearby waterfalls before continuing our journey. So the following day, we set out toward the falls.

What a remarkable sight! The mountain stream plunged down into a deep gorge that was lined with coal-black rock. It thundered into the pit, then brimmed over and roared down the mountainside. A thick curtain of mist rose up, soaking everything. We stood near the edge and peered down at the breaking water far below.

A path with an excellent view wound halfway around the falls. But it came to a dead end, so we had to go back the same way we had come out. As we retraced our steps, a messenger ran toward us with a letter in his hand. The letter said that a dying guest at the hotel had asked to see an English doctor. Could I possibly return at once?

It was a request I could hardly refuse. Holmes agreed to keep the messenger as a companion until I returned, so I started back toward the hotel. Once, when I looked back, I saw Holmes's tall figure walking rapidly along the path. Then I hurried away on my errand.

The hotel owner was standing on the porch when I arrived. "Well," I said, "where is the dying guest?" His puzzled look sent a chill down my spine. "You did not write this?" I asked, pulling out the letter. "Is no one dying?"

"Certainly not!" he cried. "This must have been written by that tall Englishman who arrived after you left. He said—"

I did not wait for him to finish. I was already running down the village street toward the mountain path. It had taken me over an hour to come down. It took me two hours to climb back up. And all I could think of was that the tall figure on the path had not been Holmes, but Moriarty!

Holmes's walking stick was leaning against the rock where he had stood, but Holmes was no longer there. I called out, but received no answer. As I looked about, I began to see what had happened.

Holmes and I had walked halfway to the end of the path. But now two sets of footprints continued past that point—and none returned.

Near the end of the path were signs of a struggle. The grass at the edge of the cliff had been pulled out by the roots. I leaned over, and my eyes followed the steep walls down to the churning water far below. Again I shouted my friend's name, but the only answer was the thunder of the falls. Holmes was gone forever.

As I sadly walked back, something caught my eye. It was Holmes's silver cigarette case. Beneath it, he had left this note.

My Dear Watson:
Moriarty is here. The letter that lured you away was written by him. I suspected as much and allowed you to go back for your own safety.

It pleases me to think that at last I will be able to free London of this evil criminal—even though it will cost me my own life as well. The evidence needed to convict his gang is in my desk at Baker Street. I am,

Very sincerely yours,
Sherlock Holmes

Little remains to be told. Professor Moriarty's gang was convicted. An official inspection confirmed that Moriarty and Holmes had struggled, then tumbled off the cliff together. Their bodies were never recovered. Even now, deep below the swirling waters of the falls, lie the bones of two men: the master criminal known as Professor Moriarty, and the greatest detective who ever lived—Sherlock Holmes.